D1164651

Zach Makes Mistakes

William Mulcahy

illustrated by
Darren McKee

free spirit
PUBLISHING®

Text copyright © 2016 by William Mulcahy
Illustrations copyright © 2016 by Free Spirit Publishing Inc.

All rights reserved under International and Pan-American Copyright Conventions. Unless otherwise noted, no part of this book may be reproduced, stored in a retrieval system, or transmitted in any form or by any means, electronic, mechanical, photocopying, recording, or otherwise, without express written permission of the publisher, except for brief quotations or critical reviews. For more information, go to www.freespirit.com/permissions.

Free Spirit, Free Spirit Publishing, and associated logos are trademarks and/or registered trademarks of Free Spirit Publishing Inc. A complete listing of our logos and trademarks is available at www.freespirit.com.

Library of Congress Cataloging-in-Publication Data
Names: Mulcahy, William, author. | McKee, Darren, illustrator.
Title: Zach makes mistakes / William Mulcahy ; illustrated by Darren McKee.
Description: Golden Valley : Free Spirit Publishing Inc., 2016. | Series: Zach rules
Identifiers: LCCN 2016002904 | ISBN 9781631981104 (hard cover) | ISBN 1631981102 (hard cover) | ISBN 9781631981111 (Web pdf) |
    ISBN 9781631981128 (epub)
Subjects: LCSH: Errors—Juvenile literature.
Classification: LCC BF323.E7 .M85 2016 | DDC 395.1/22—dc23
LC record available at http://lccn.loc.gov/2016002904

Free Spirit Publishing does not have control over or assume responsibility for author or third-party websites and their content.

Reading Level Grade 3; Interest Level Ages 5–8;
Fountas & Pinnell Guided Reading Level N

Edited by Eric Braun
Cover and interior design by Tasha Kenyon

10 9 8 7 6 5 4 3 2 1
Printed in the United States of America
B10950516

Free Spirit Publishing Inc.
6325 Sandburg Road, Suite 100
Minneapolis, MN 55427-3674
(612) 338-2068
help4kids@freespirit.com
www.freespirit.com

Free Spirit offers competitive pricing.
Contact edsales@freespirit.com for pricing information on multiple quantity purchases.

Dedication

To Melissa, for showing me, and embracing with me,
the music and the dance to its fullest. It's truly never too late
to become the person you want to be. I love you.

Acknowledgments

For all of your support of the adventures of Zach, my deep gratitude to:

Aimee Jackson, for her guidance, wisdom, and incredible gift of faith.

My colleagues at Lighthouse Counseling, especially Jane Sweney, for suggestions toward the section for adults.

Eric Braun, an incredible editor whom I am honored to have working on my side.

And lastly, to my six children: Liam, Luke, Kegen, Jack, Makenna, and Masen, for your energy, playfulness, and ongoing curiosity about everything Zach.

CONCORDIA UNIVERSITY LIBRARY
PORTLAND, OR 97211

Zach was excited for his class field trip to the museum. He could hardly wait to see the bison display! But as he walked into his classroom, he realized he had made a big mistake.

1

Oh, no! He had forgotten to wear his orange school shirt. Students were supposed to wear them on field trips.

He asked his teacher, Ms. Rosamond, if he could call his mom. His teacher let him use her cell phone. But Zach's mom was already at work. "Sorry," Mom said. "I can't bring your T-shirt to school."

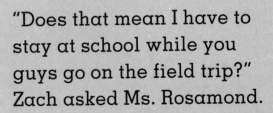

"Does that mean I have to stay at school while you guys go on the field trip?" Zach asked Ms. Rosamond.

"No," Ms. Rosamond said. "I have an extra shirt—it's a little big, but it's better than nothing."

Zach's best friend, Sonya, tried to cheer him up. "Everyone makes mistakes," she said.

"Easy for you to say," Zach said. "You're not wearing a big ugly tent to the field trip."

Sonya told Zach about the time she made a huge mistake by dressing up for her friend's birthday party in a Halloween costume instead of her dress-up clothes. "I thought dress up meant wearing a costume."

Zach laughed thinking about Sonya wearing a costume at a fancy party. By the time they got to the museum, he felt a little better.

5

Before they went inside, Ms. Rosamond reminded everyone to listen to the guide. "Be polite, listen carefully, and don't interrupt," she said.

Museum Rules
1. Keep hands off displays.
2. Please silence all phones.

The guide's name was Tim. He told them about some of the cool exhibits they would see that day. He also reminded them to follow the rules.

Suddenly, a cell phone rang. "I'm so sorry!" Ms. Rosamond said, reaching into her purse. She quickly turned it off.

Zach felt embarrassed for her.

When the presentation ended, Ms. Rosamond talked to Tim. "I'm really sorry about that," she said. "I forgot to turn off my phone."

Tim told her it was okay.

The museum was even more awesome than Zach thought it would be. He saw moon rocks.

He saw Blackfoot Indian clothing and a collection of weird bugs and butterflies.

Best of all, he saw American bison running across a prairie. The bison looked so alive and soft, he reached across the rope and put his hand on one of them.

"Hey!" Tim called.
"No touching!"

Zach pulled his hand back. How embarrassing! He wished he could hide in a closet until the trip was over.

When it was time for lunch, Zach sat next to Ms. Rosamond. "I feel awful when I mess up," he confided.

"I know what you mean," his teacher replied. "When I forgot to turn off my phone, I felt pretty foolish."

Zach nodded.

"But," she went on, "I have learned to deal with my mistakes and move on."

"I wish I could learn to move on. How do you do it?"

Ms. Rosamond smiled and showed him what was on her necklace. "This is the Key to Mistakes. Take a look."

Three words were engraved on the loops of the handle: **Detect, Correct, Reflect.** The stem of the key had words, too: **Nobody's Perfect.**

Ms. Rosamond said, "When I was young, mistakes made me feel really bad, like I was a failure. My grandma helped me see how to learn from mistakes and feel better about them. Then she had this key made to help me remember."

Zach laughed. It sounded like something his dad would have taught him.

"The first thing is to **detect** your mistake—to find the reason for it," Ms. Rosamond said. "Mistakes are made by not understanding something, by not paying attention, or by not being careful. Which was the reason for your mistake?"

"I wasn't paying attention when I didn't put on the school shirt. I also wasn't paying attention when I broke the no-touching rule."

14

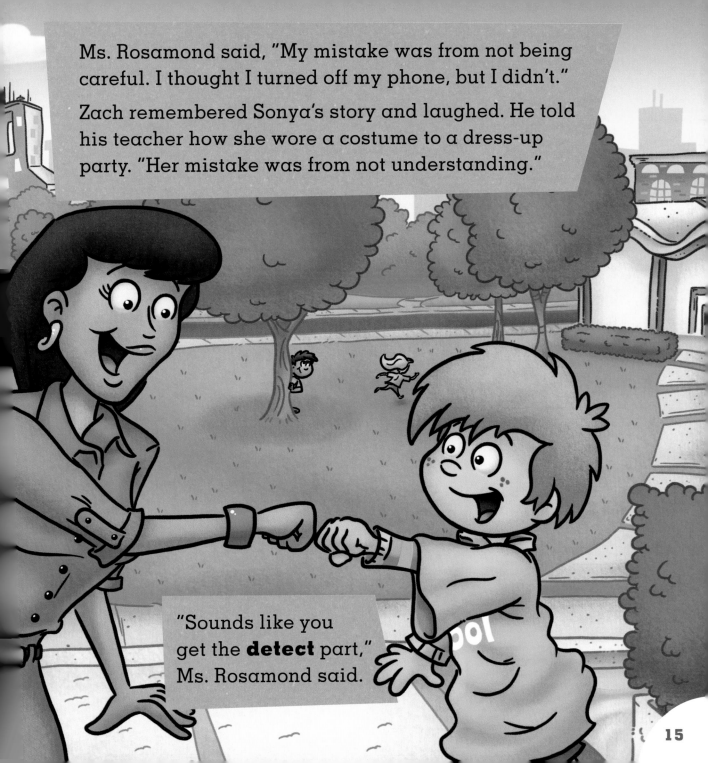

Ms. Rosamond said, "My mistake was from not being careful. I thought I turned off my phone, but I didn't."

Zach remembered Sonya's story and laughed. He told his teacher how she wore a costume to a dress-up party. "Her mistake was from not understanding."

"Sounds like you get the **detect** part," Ms. Rosamond said.

Ms. Rosamond said, "The next loop on the key says **'Correct.'**"

Zach said, "When Tim told me 'No touching,' I stopped."

"Exactly. And when my phone rang, I turned it off right away. And I apologized to Tim. There are lots of ways to **correct** a mistake."

"But wait," Zach said. "When I tried to call my mom to bring my shirt, she was already at work. I couldn't fix that mistake." He looked down at his huge orange shirt. "At least you found this," he said.

"Sometimes you can't fix a mistake, but it's important to try," his teacher said. "And sometimes you need a little help."

"The last loop on the key says **'Reflect,'**" Ms. Rosamond said. "That means to look back on your mistake and think about it."

"When I look back on my mistakes, I feel awful," Zach said. "I try to forget them."

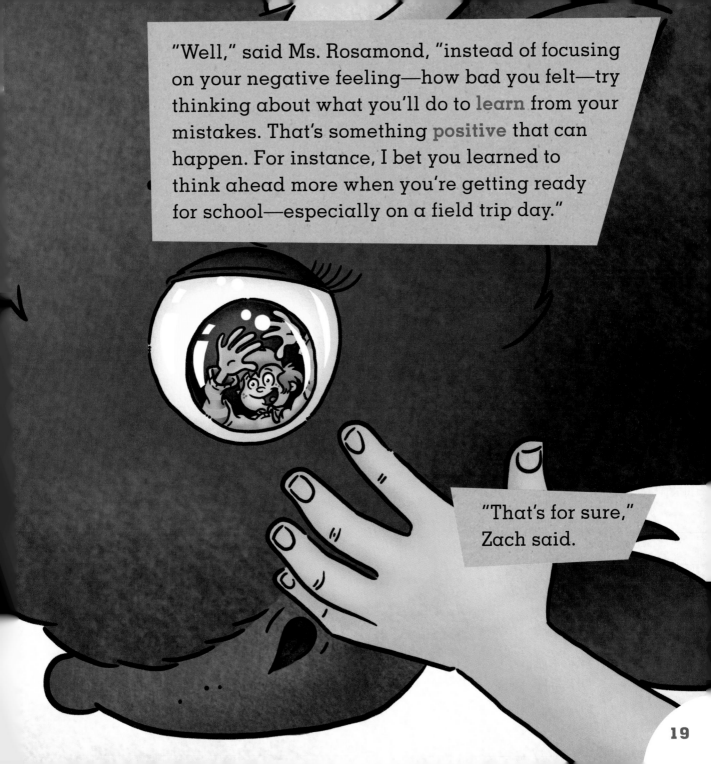

"Well," said Ms. Rosamond, "instead of focusing on your negative feeling—how bad you felt—try thinking about what you'll do to learn from your mistakes. That's something positive that can happen. For instance, I bet you learned to think ahead more when you're getting ready for school—especially on a field trip day."

"That's for sure," Zach said.

"Is there anything left?"
Ms. Rosamond asked.

Zach read the stem of the key:
"Nobody's Perfect."

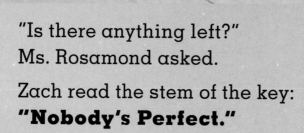

METEORITE

Sea Room

Ms. Rosamond said, "My grandma put that there to remind me that everyone makes mistakes and not to be too hard on myself."

Zach said, "One time my dad took my brother and me to the movies. We got all the way there and he realized he forgot his wallet. Big mistake!"

"Adults make as many mistakes as kids," Ms. Rosamond said. "Probably more! The key is not to let them get you down."

22

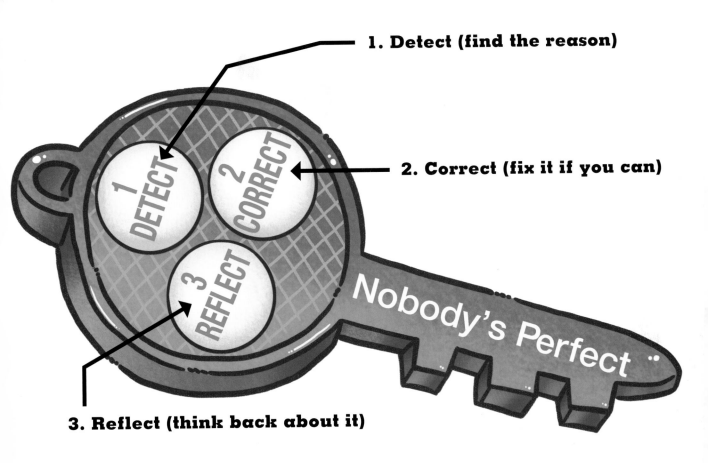

1. Detect (find the reason)

2. Correct (fix it if you can)

3. Reflect (think back about it)

To help you learn from your mistakes, you can use Ms. Rosamond's **Key to Mistakes**. **Detect** your mistake by figuring out why you made it. **Correct** your mistake by trying to fix the wrong you did. **Reflect** on your mistake by thinking about what you learned. How can you do better next time? Not only will the **Key to Mistakes** help you learn from your mistakes, it will help you remember that Nobody's Perfect—including yourself.

Helping Children Learn from Mistakes

Mistakes can be embarrassing, frustrating—even infuriating. Some mistakes can ruin your whole day. This is as true for grown-ups as it is for kids. But while most adults have the skills and experience to handle mistakes in an emotionally healthy way, young children typically need our help learning to overcome their mistakes and grow from them.

Because mistakes can feel so uncomfortable, many children fear making them and try to be perfect. Other kids may appear to have a casual attitude toward mistakes, repeating the same ones over and over and not seeming to learn anything from them. Most kids fall somewhere in between—they simply do their best to get over their mistakes and move on. In any case, children's success at learning from mistakes depends on their ability to handle the emotional fallout that comes with making them. That's where the Key to Mistakes comes in. It's a tool that puts kids in charge of their emotions and behavior, providing a skill that gives them a foundation for a lifetime of learning and growth.

The Key to Mistakes is a three-part process that helps kids develop the awareness to recognize their mistakes and the control to handle the gritty emotions that often accompany them. This proactive approach to mistakes enables lessons to emerge, creating a positive outcome from something that at first feels only negative.

The Key to Mistakes is most successful when children and adults are partners in learning and practicing the steps. As you work together with kids, always keep in mind two things: nobody's perfect and everybody makes mistakes. These phrases may seem cliché, but they're true, and they're truly important! Approach children who have made mistakes with compassion, empathy, and an eye on learning from this situation. When you model this attitude, you show children how to treat themselves that way, too.

The Key to Mistakes has the power to:

- Teach valuable life lessons and consequences
- Teach us about our strengths and weaknesses
- Teach us how to forgive ourselves
- Decrease fear and anxiety about making mistakes
- Help us learn, grow, and evolve
- Help us understand we are not perfect—and that's okay
- Help us take responsibility and feel empowered

Here is more information about the three parts of the Key to Mistakes and some tips to help guide your child:

1. **Detect.** In this step, children are asked to admit their mistake and discover why they made it. Help them figure out whether their mistake came from not understanding something, not paying attention, or not being careful. Don't underestimate the power of this first step. The awareness that comes from admitting a mistake and discovering the reason behind it puts children in a stronger position to cope with their current and future emotions and behaviors. By honestly detecting their mistake, children are learning to pay closer attention, practice deeper understanding, and be more careful.

2. **Correct.** In this step, children look for ways to fix their mistake or make things better. Some mistakes are easier to fix than others. If a child forgets to pick up her toys, she can fix things by picking them up right away. Other mistakes may require more effort. If someone has been hurt or offended, an apology is probably appropriate. Some mistakes need help from an adult to fix. Encourage and coach children to find solutions on their own, but don't hesitate to assist if needed. However kids can fix their mistake, they benefit greatly both cognitively and emotionally from the experience. Even if a mistake cannot be fixed, the act of *trying* to fix it is valuable.

3. **Reflect.** In this step, children are given time to think back over their mistakes, learn from them, and make peace with themselves if they need to. At first, kids may need extra coaching on this step. It's not always easy to see the "lesson" in a bad day or painful moment. Help them out by asking questions like, "What might you do differently in the future?" and "What do you know now that you didn't know before?" Remind kids that they are growing and learning every day. They're smarter now than they were before the mistake!

Nobody's Perfect is more than a step. It's a gentle reminder that connects all of us in our humanity. It's a reminder to be compassionate and understanding with others and ourselves. And it's a reminder that everybody makes mistakes—but we also have the power and responsibility to grow from these mistakes.

A few other tips:

- Never shame, intimidate, or badger a child for a making a mistake, and don't punish kids for mistakes. Once a mistake has been detected, corrected, and reflected, let it go.

- However, feel free to remind kids of a past mistake that they overcame in a positive way. Such reminders can help a child deal with a current tough situation or avoid future mistakes.

- Teach children to pay attention to how it feels in their bodies to make mistakes. This is valuable information that children can use in the future to see mistakes as they're coming and to further their learning. When a child made a mistake, did his face feel warm? Did her stomach get tight or stirred up? Teach self-relaxation skills such as deep breathing, counting to ten, and visualization to help a child cope with these body feelings.

- Ask children to adopt a curious, nonjudgmental attitude when working through their mistakes. You can say, "Be kind to yourself. A mistake doesn't mean you're bad. It's a chance to learn. How can you do better next time?" This helps them focus on learning from their mistakes instead of shaming themselves.

- If you are concerned about your child's ability to deal with making mistakes, please seek professional help.

Parents hate to see their kids experience pain or setbacks, but these are how children learn and grow. We can't prevent them from making mistakes, and we shouldn't try to. Instead, celebrate mistakes. Use the Key to Mistakes to turn a negative experience into a positive, enriching one.

Download a printable copy of Ms. Rosamond's Key to Mistakes at www.freespirit.com/Mistakes.

About the Author

William Mulcahy is a licensed professional counselor and psychotherapist. He has served as supervisor at Family Service of Waukesha and as a counselor at Stillwaters Cancer Support Center in Wisconsin, specializing in grief and cancer-related issues, and he has worked with children with special needs. Currently he works in private practice in Pewaukee, Wisconsin, and is the owner of Kids Cope Now, a program for providing books and tools to help kids in the hospital. Bill's picture books include *Zach Apologizes*, *Zach Gets Frustrated*, and *Zoey Goes to the Hospital*. He lives in Summit, Wisconsin, with three children, three stepchildren, and his wife Melissa in a home where life is never boring. His website is kidscopenow.com.

About the Illustrator

Darren McKee has illustrated books for many publishers over his 20-year career. When not working, he spends his time riding his bike, reading, drawing, and traveling. He lives in Dallas, Texas, with his wife Debbie.

More Great Books from Free Spirit

Zach Rules Series

by William Mulcahy, illustrated by Darren McKee

Zach struggles with social issues like getting along, handling frustrations, making mistakes, and other everyday problems typical of young kids. Each book in the Zach Rules series presents a single, simple storyline involving one such problem. As each story develops, Zach and readers learn straightforward tools for coping with their struggles and building stronger relationships now and in the future.
Each book: 32 pp., color illust., HC, 8¼" x 8¼", ages 5–8.

Penelope Perfect
A Tale of Perfectionism Gone Wild
by Shannon Anderson, illustrated by Katie Kath

48 pp., color illust., PB & HC, 8" x 10", ages 5–9.

Coasting Casey
A Tale of Busting Boredom in School
by Shannon Anderson, illustrated by Colleen Madden

48 pp., color illust., PB & HC, 8" x 10", ages 5–9.

Interested in purchasing multiple quantities and receiving volume discounts?
Contact edsales@freespirit.com or call 1.800.735.7323 and ask for Education Sales.

Many Free Spirit authors are available for speaking engagements, workshops, and keynotes.
Contact speakers@freespirit.com or call 1.800.735.7323.

For pricing information, to place an order, or to request a free catalog, contact:

free spirit PUBLISHING®

6325 Sandburg Road • Suite 100 • Golden Valley, MN 55427-3674
toll-free 800.735.7323 • local 612.338.2068 • fax 612.337.5050
help4kids@freespirit.com • www.freespirit.com

C.Lit BF 323 .E7 .M85 2016
Mulcahy, William,
Zach makes mistakes